KIDNAPPED

Robert Louis Stevenson

adapted by
Deborah Kestel

ABDO
Publishing Company

GREAT ILLUSTRATED CLASSICS

edited by
Malvina G. Vogel

visit us at
www.abdopub.com

Library edition published in 2002 by ABDO Publishing Company, 4940 Viking Drive, Suite 622, Edina, Minnesota 55435. Published by agreement with Playmore Incorporated Publishers and Waldman Publishing Corporation.

Printed in the United States.

Library of Congress Cataloging-in-Publication Data

Stevenson, Robert Louis, 1850-1894.
    Kidnapped / Robert Louis Stevenson ; adapted by Deborah Kestel.
       p. cm – (Great illustrated classics)
    Reprint. Originally published: New York: Playmore: Waldman Pub., 1992.
    Summary: In 1751 in Scotland, cheated out of his inheritance by a greedy uncle who has him kidnapped and put on a ship to the Carolinas, seventeen-year-old David Balfour escapes to the Highlands with the help of the Jacobite Alan Breck Stewart and there encounters further danger and intrigue as he attempts to clear his name and regain his property.
    ISBN 1-57765-690-3
    1. Scotland--History--18th century--Juvenile fiction. [1. Scotland--History--18th century--Fiction. 2. Adventure and adventurers--Fiction. 3. Coming of age--Fiction.] I. Kestal, Deborah. II. Title. III. Series.

PZ7.S8482 Ki 2002
[Fic]--dc21

                                                                                    2001055388

CONTENTS

About the Author

Robert Louis Stevenson was born in Edinburgh, Scotland. He was often sick as a child and spent many days reading at home because he couldn't attend classes. His work was to be interrupted by illness all his life.

He entered the University when he was seventeen. His parents thought he would be a civil engineer like his father, who followed the family profession of lighthouse engineer. Stevenson did study some law, but was soon drawn to travel by his love for the sea and open air.

Stevenson used his experiences in his books. He traveled widely—to England, France, Switzerland, across the United States, and on through the South Sea islands.

In France, he went on a long canoe trip inland with his cousin. In California, he lived in a rough mining camp for a year. He knew a great deal of Scottish history from his reading as a child and used it as background for some of his tales.

For six years, he traveled the South Pacific in *Casco,* a schooner yacht. Visiting Tahiti, Hawaii, Australia and Samoa, he came to know the islanders better than any writer of his time.

When he was forty, he decided to stop his wandering, and he built a home in Samoa. He named the house Vailina, which means Five Rivers.

He spent the rest of his life in Samoa, where he became a planter and a politician. Because of all the interest he took in their lives, the Samoans built a road to his house and called it "The Road of the Loving Heart."

Characters You Will Meet

David Balfour   *a lad of seventeen*
Mr. Campbell   *the minister in Essendean*
Ebenezer Balfour   *David's wicked uncle*
Ransome   *the cabin boy*
Hoseason   *the captain of the* Covenant
Mr. Riach   *mate on the* Covenant
Mr. Shuan   *mate on the* Covenant
Alan Breck Stewart   *the man with the belt of gold*
Neil Ray Macrob   *the ferryman*
Mr. Henderland   *a clergyman*
Colin Roy Campbell   *the Red Fox*
James Stewart   *a member of Alan's clan*
John Breck Maccoll   *Alan's friend*
Cluny Macpherson   *chief of the Macpherson clan*
Robin Oig Campbell   *another fugitive*
Lass from Stirling   *a helpful waitress*
Mr. Rankeillor   *the lawyer in Edinburgh*

David Begins His Adventures.

Chapter 1

I Set Off Upon My Journey

My adventures began early one June morning in the year 1751. I was a lad of seventeen. I locked the door of my father's house for the last time. The sun shone on the hilltops as I went down the road.

Mr. Campbell, the minister, was waiting for me by his garden gate.

"Well, Davie lad," said he, "I will go with you to the river, to start you on your way."

We began to walk in silence.

"Are ye sorry to leave Essendean?" he asked.

"Essendean is a good place," said I, "but I have never been anywhere else."

"Well, Davie," said Mr. Campbell, "when your mother was gone and your father was dying, he gave me this letter and told me to give you the letter and send you to the house of Shaws, where he came from."

"The house of Shaws!" I cried. "What had my poor father to do with the house of Shaws?"

"Who can tell?" said Mr. Campbell. "The name of that family, Davie boy, is your name—Balfour of Shaws."

The letter was addressed: "To the hands of Ebenezer Balfour, of Shaws, these will be delivered by my son, David Balfour." My heart was beating hard.

"Mr. Campbell," I stammered, "if you were in my shoes, would you go?"

"Ay, I would," said the minister.

He gave me a little packet, then embraced

"The House of Shaws!"

me very hard, looking like he was about to cry. He turned away quickly, crying goodbye, and set off at a jogging run. I watched him as long as I could. He never stopped hurrying, nor once looked back.

He had given me a small Bible, a shilling, and a recipe for Lily of the Valley water. That recipe was to help me wonderfully in health and sickness all my life.

I was sad to leave my good friend, but glad to set out on my way. When I came to the green road up the side of the hill, I took my last look at the Essendean church and the trees in the yard where my father and mother lay buried.

Sad to Leave

First View of the Sea

Chapter 2

I Come to My Journey's End

On the afternoon of the second day, I saw all the countryside before me fall away down to the sea. There were ships in the inlet and a flag upon the castle at Edinburgh. It was my first view of the sea, and I stood in wonder for some time.

I began to ask directions to the house of Shaws. The folk I asked looked at me strangely. One honest fellow told me that Shaws was a big house with only Mr. Ebenezer in it. "And mannie," he added, "it's none of my affairs, but ye seem a decent-spoken lad. If ye take my word, ye'll keep clear of the Shaws."

What sort of house, or man, could make the countryfolk so uneasy? If I had been closer to Essendean, I would have turned back.

Near sundown, I reached the house of Shaws. This was no great house. It appeared to be in ruin. No road led up to it. No smoke rose from any of the chimneys. My heart sank.

I walked through the grass past two stone pillars, a main entrance gate that was never finished. One wing of the house had no roof, and steps and stairs showed against the sky. Some of the windows had no glass, and bats flew in and out.

I lifted my hand with a faint heart and knocked once on the door. Then I stood and waited. No one answered.

I began to shout aloud for Mr. Balfour. Then I heard a cough right overhead. I

No Great House

jumped back and looking up, saw a man's head in a tall nightcap and the wide mouth of a blunderbuss at a window.

"It's loaded," said a voice.

"I have come with a letter," I said, "to Mr. Balfour of Shaws. Is he here?"

"Who are ye yourself?"

"They call me David Balfour," said I.

I heard the blunderbuss rattle on the windowsill. After a long pause, with a curious change of voice, he asked, "Is your father dead?"

I was so surprised I could not answer, but stood staring.

"He must be dead, that's what brings you knocking at my door. Well, man," he said, "I'll let ye in."

"It's Loaded!"

A Bare Room

Chapter 3

I Meet My Uncle

Soon there came a great rattling of chains and bolts. The door was opened slowly and shut again behind me.

"Go into the kitchen and touch nothing," said the voice.

I came to the barest room I ever laid eyes on. There was nothing in the great stone chamber but a table set for a poor supper, a few dishes on a shelf, and locked chests along the wall.

The man joined me. He was a mean, stooping, clay-faced creature, and his age was

KIDNAPPED

anything between fifty and seventy. He wore a flannel nightcap and nightgown, and he was unshaved.

"Let's see the letter," said he.

I told him the letter was for Mr. Balfour, the lord of Shaws.

"Hoot-toot! And who do ye think I am?" he said. "Give me Alexander's letter!"

"You know my father's name?"

"It would be strange if I didn't," he said. "He was my brother. I'm your uncle, Davie, my man. Give us the letter, and sit down and eat."

There was only one bite of porridge left. This was no rich house, and my uncle was no great lord. I was so disappointed I almost cried.

"Your father's been long dead?" he asked.

"Three weeks, sir," said I. "I never knew he had a brother till you told me."

22

David's Uncle Reads the Letter.

KIDNAPPED

He lit no lamp on the steps as he showed me my bed. I stumbled after him in the dark.

"Lights in a house are a thing I do not like. Good night to ye." He pulled the door shut and locked me in.

The room was cold as a well and the bed was damp. I rolled myself in my plaid and slept on the floor.

When I woke, I was cold and miserable. I could see that only spiders and mice used the room now. I knocked and shouted till my jailer came and let me out.

At breakfast, he asked me about my mother and said she had been a bonnie lassie. I was surprised to hear that he knew her.

My uncle kept a close eye on me. I was sure he didn't like me or trust me.

Ebenezer Locks David In.

Ebenezer Grabs David's Jacket.

Chapter 4

I Run a Great Danger

In a room next to the kitchen, where he let me go, I found a great number of books in Latin and English. On the first page in one book, I found this written by my father's hand: "To my brother Ebenezer on his fifth birthday." I was puzzled. The eldest son Ebenezer had inherited the house, so my father was the younger brother. But a child younger than five could not have written so neatly.

When I asked my uncle if perhaps they were twins, he jumped at me and grabbed my jacket.

"Stop it, David," he said, "ye should not speak to me about your father."

I began to think my uncle was insane and dangerous. I also thought of the ballad of a poor lad whose wicked kinsman tried to keep land that was the lad's.

That night my uncle asked me to go to the stair tower at the far end of the house. He wanted a chest of papers that was at the top of the tower.

"Can I have a light, sir?" said I.

"Nae," said he, very cunningly. "Nae lights in my house."

"Are the stairs good?"

"They're grand," said he. "Keep to the wall. There's no bannister, but the stairs are good underfoot."

Out I went into the night. The wind was moaning in the distance, though never a breath of it came near the house of Shaws.

"Nae Light."

KIDNAPPED

Night had fallen blacker than ever. I felt along the wall till I came to the stair tower door at the far end of the unfinished wing.

It was so dark inside the tower that I felt I could hardly breathe. I kept close to the tower side and felt my way in the pitch darkness with a beating heart. I went up the stairs on my hands and knees as slowly as a snail.

The house of Shaws was five stories high. I had come to one of the turns in the stairway, when, feeling forward as usual, my hand slipped over an edge and found nothing but emptiness beyond it. A sudden blink of summer lightning showed me I had been climbing on an open scaffold. The tower had never been finished. I was so full of fear my cry stuck in my throat. If I had taken another step, I would have fallen and died.

I turned and felt my way down again with a great anger in my heart. About halfway

Up the Stair Tower

down, the wind sprang up in a clap and shook the tower and then died again. The rain followed.

Perhaps my uncle thought the crash of thunder was the sound of my fall. I found him in a fit of panic fear. He was shuddering and groaning aloud.

"Are ye alive?" he sobbed. "O man, are ye alive?"

"That I am," said I. "Small thanks to you!"

I set him on a chair and looked at him. I demanded to know why he lied to me.

"I'll tell ye in the morn," he said. "As sure as death I will."

He was so weak I could do nothing but agree. I locked him in his room. Then I made a big fire in the kitchen and fell asleep.

In a Fit of Panic Fear

A Half-Grown Boy in Sea-Clothes

Chapter 5

I Go to the Queen's Ferry

There was now no doubt that my uncle was my enemy. I feared he might do anything to harm me.

After I had let him out of his room, I asked, "Why do you fear me, cheat me, and try to kill me?" I saw by his face he had no lie ready for me, though he was hard at work thinking of one. We were interrupted by a knocking at the door.

I found on the doorstep a half-grown boy in sea-clothes. He was blue with the cold.

"What cheer, mate?" said he, with a

cracked voice. "I've brought a letter from old Heasyoasy to Mr. Belflower. And I say, mate, I'm hungry."

"Well," said I, "come in and you shall have a bite if I go empty for it."

He fell-to greedily on the remains of breakfast while my uncle read the letter. Soon my uncle looked up at me and said, "I have business with this man Hoseason, captain of the *Covenant,* the trading brig. If you and me was to walk over with yon lad, I could see the captain in town, or maybe on board the *Covenant,* and then we could jog on to the lawyer, Mr. Rankeillor's. He's lawyer for half the gentlemen in these parts, and he knew your father."

I stood awhile and thought. My uncle would not harm me if many people were near. And here was a chance to meet someone who could tell me the story of my family, a man who had known my father. I also wished a

The Boy Eats the Remains of Breakfast.

closer view of the sea and ships, which I had seen for the first time in my life just two days before.

While we walked, I talked to the cabin boy, Ransome. He had gone to sea at nine and couldn't say how old he was now. He showed me tattoo marks and boasted of many wild and bad things he had done. I pitied him more than I believed him.

He ran on about Heasyoasy, as he called the captain, and told me of a Mr. Shuan, a mate who beat him sometimes and gave him brandy. Then he talked of the unhappy criminals who were sent overseas on ships like the *Covenant* to slavery in North America, and the more unhappy innocent men who were kidnapped and taken to America to be sold for money.

Just then we came to the top of the hill. The placed looked pretty lonely. There were not many people about. A small boat was at

Walking with Ransome, the Cabin Boy

the pier. Some seamen were asleep in it. Ransome told me this was the brig's boat waiting for the captain. He pointed out the *Covenant* herself, at anchor about half a mile out. There was a seagoing bustle on board; yards were swinging into place. I could hear the song of the sailors as they pulled upon the ropes. After all that I had listened to on the way, I looked at that ship very uncomfortably, and I pitied all the poor souls that had to sail in her.

I decided that nothing could make me board the *Covenant.*

A Pretty Lonely Place

The Ship Captain

Chapter 6

What Happened at the Queen's Ferry

As we came to the inn, Ransome led us up the stair to a small room that was heated like an oven by a great fire of coal. At a table close by the chimney, a tall, dark, stern man sat writing. I never saw any man look cooler or more studious than this ship captain.

"I am proud to see you, Mr. Balfour," said he, offering his large hand to Ebenezer. They sat down to a bottle and a great mass of papers. Although I had promised myself not to let my uncle out of sight, I was impatient for a look at the sea. The room was so hot that when my uncle said, "Go out by yourself awhile," I was fool enough to do so.

The smell of seawater was very salty and stirring. The *Covenant* was beginning to shake out her sails, and I thought of far voyages and foreign places. I looked at the seamen—big brown fellows, some in shirts, some with jackets, some with colored handkerchiefs, some with heavy clubs. All had knives. I talked with one of them, then returned to the inn with Ransome.

The landlord there began talking about Ebenezer. He told us of the rumor that he had killed his brother Alexander, who was my father. This interested me.

"And what would he kill him for?" said I.

"To get the place," said he. "Alexander was the eldest son."

I sat stunned with my good fortune and could scarcely believe that the same poor lad who had walked from Essendean only two

The Seamen Wait.

days ago was now rich. The house of Shaws belonged to me by right of birth. It was a pleasant thought.

I heard a voice calling me. It was the captain, who invited me aboard his brig to drink a bowl. Now, I longed to see the inside of a ship more than words can tell. But I was not going to put myself in danger, so I told him my uncle and I had an appointment with a lawyer.

The captain passed an arm through mine and leaning down, warned me about the schemes of my uncle. I thought (poor fool that I was!) that I had found a good friend and helper, and began to doubt Ransome's stories about this fine man.

My uncle, the captain and I joined the men in the boat that would take us to the ship. Hoseason declared that he and I must be the first aboard. I was whipped into the air on a tackle sent down from the mainyard and set

A New Friend?

on deck. I was a little dizzy as the ship rolled, perhaps a little afraid, yet very pleased with the strange sights.

"But where is my uncle?" said I suddenly.

"Ay," said Hoseason, with a sudden grimness, "that's the point."

I felt I was lost. I gave a piercing cry, "Help! Help! Murder!"

I saw my uncle sitting in the stern of the boat pulling back to the dock. His face was full of cruelty and terror.

It was the last I saw. Strong hands held me. A thunderbolt seemed to strike me, and I fell senseless.

Strong Hands Hold David.

Awakened by a Small Man

Chapter 7

I Go to Sea in the Brig *Covenant*

I came to in darkness, in great pain, and bound hand and foot. I lay somewhere in the belly of that unlucky ship. The whole world heaved up, then rushed down. I could hear the scurryings of the ship's rats that sometimes ran across my face. I was sick and hurt, confused, angry and miserable. I fainted again.

I was awakened by the light of a hand-lantern shining in my face. A small man of about thirty, with green eyes, stood looking down at me.

"Well," said he, "how goes it?"

I answered with a sob. He felt my pulse and forehead, and washed and dressed the wound on my scalp. My head was swimming and filled with a horrid giddiness.

The man with the green eyes left and returned with the captain.

"I want that boy taken out of this hole and put in the forecastle," the man said.

"Here he is, here he shall stay, Mr. Riach," returned the captain.

"The lad will die," said Mr. Riach.

Hoseason grumbled, "Put him where ye please!" and climbed the ladder. My ropes were cut, and I was carried on a man's back to the forecastle.

It was a blessed thing to open my eyes the next day to daylight and to find myself among other men. The forecastle was a roomy place. It was set all about with berths, in which the men who were not on duty were

Carried to Daylight

seated smoking, or lying down asleep. One of the men brought me a drink of something healing which Mr. Riach had prepared and told me to lie still.

Here I lay for many days and came to know my companions. They were a rough lot. Some of them had sailed with pirates and seen things that should not be spoken. The ship was bound for the Carolinas, where white men were still sold into slavery on the plantations. My wicked uncle had sold me to Hoseason for a slave.

Ransome came in at times from the roundhouse, sometimes nursing a bruise from Mr. Shuan. Ransome also drank, and he talked of his father, who had made clocks and kept a bird in the parlor. In his years of hardships, he had forgotten his childhood. He seemed such an unhappy, friendless boy.

A Rough Lot

A Shipmate with Stories

Chapter 8

Aboard the *Covenant*

No class of man is altogether bad, but each has its own faults and virtues. These shipmates of mine were no exception to the rule. They were rough and bad, I suppose, but they had many virtues. They were kind when it occurred to them, simple even beyond the simplicity of a country lad like me, and had some glimmerings of honesty.

There was one man, of maybe forty, who would sit for hours and tell me of his wife and child. He was a fisherman who had lost his boat and thus been driven to deep sea voyaging.

KIDNAPPED

His wife waited in vain to see her man return, but he would never again make the fire for her in the morning, nor take care of the child when she was sick. Indeed, many of these poor fellows (as the event proved) were upon their last cruise; the deep seas and cannibal fish received them.

I did my best in the small time allowed me to make friends with the unfriended creature, Ransome. But his mind was hardly human. He had strange ideas about the dry land, picked up from sailor's stories. He thought it was a place where lads were put to some kind of slavery called a trade, and where apprentices were beaten and clapped into foul prisons. In a town, he thought every third house was a place where seamen would be drugged and murdered. I would tell him how kindly I had been treated on that dry land he was so afraid of, and how well fed and carefully taught by my friends and parents. If he had

David Befriends Ransome.

been recently hurt, he would weep bitterly and swear to run away. But if he was in his usual crackbrain humor, or if he had had a glass of spirits in the roundhouse, he would laugh at the idea of living on land.

It was Mr. Riach who gave the boy drink. No doubt he meant it kindly, but it was a pitiful thing to see this poor creature staggering, and dancing, and talking he knew not what. Some of the men laughed, but not all. Others would grow as black as thunder, thinking, perhaps, of their own childhood or their own children. They bid him stop that nonsense and think what he was doing. As for me, I felt ashamed to look at him.

All this time, the *Covenant* was meeting continual headwinds and tumbling up and down against headseas, so that the scuttle was almost constantly shut and the forecastle lighted only by a swinging lantern on a beam. There was constant labor for all hands; the

Watching Ransome Dance

sails had to be made and shortened every hour. The strain told on the men's temper. There was a growl of quarreling all day long from berth to berth. I was never allowed to set my foot on deck. I grew weary of my life and impatient for a change.

And a change I was to get, but I must first tell of a conversation I had with Mr. Riach which put a little heart in me to bear my troubles. I got him a bit drunk, pledged him to secrecy, and told him my whole story.

He declared it was like a ballad and said that he would do his best to help me.

"And in the meantime," said he, "keep your heart up. You're not the only one, I'll tell you that. There's many a man hoeing tobacco overseas that should be mounting his horse at his own door at home—many and many! Look at me. I'm a lord's son and more than half a doctor, and here I am, mate to Hoseason!"

Constant Labor for All Hands

I thought it would be civil to ask him for his story.

He whistled loud.

"Never had one," said he. "I like fun, that's all." And he skipped out of the forecastle.

Sharing Stories

Ransome's Face is White as Wax.

Chapter 9

The Roundhouse

One night, about eleven o'clock, a man of the watch came below. A whisper went about, "Shuan has done it at last." The scuttle was flung open, and Captain Hoseason came down the ladder and walked straight up to me.

"My man," said he, "we want ye to serve in the roundhouse. You and Ransome are to change berths. Run away aft with ye."

Two seamen appeared carrying Ransome in their arms. The boy's face was as white as wax and had a look on it like a dreadful smile. The blood in me ran cold. I brushed by the sailors and the boy, and ran up the ladder onto the deck.

The roundhouse, where I was now to sleep and serve, stood some six feet above the decks. Inside were a fixed table and bench and two berths, one for the captain and one for the two mates to share. There were lockers from top to bottom and a second storeroom underneath it. All the best meat and drink and all the gunpowder were there. Almost all the firearms were set in a rack on the roundhouse wall.

A small window and a skylight gave it light by day. After dark, a lamp burned.

Mr. Shuan was sitting in the lamplight at the table with the brandy bottle and a tin cup. He was a tall man, strong and very drunk.

The captain leaned on the berth beside me, staring darkly at the mate. Mr. Riach came in. He gave the captain a look that meant the

Mr. Shuan at the Table

boy was dead, caught the bottle away from Mr. Shuan, and tossed it into the sea.

Mr. Shuan was on his feet. He meant to harm Mr. Riach.

"Sit down!" roared the captain. "Ye sot and swine, do ye know what ye've done? Ye've murdered the boy!"

Mr. Shuan sat down and put up his hand to his brow.

"Well," he said, "he brought me a dirty cup."

The captain and I and Mr. Riach all looked at each other for a second with a kind of frightened look. The murderer cried a little. Then Hoseason made him take off his seaboots and go to bed.

That was the first night of my new duties. I had to serve at meals and be at the call of the three men always. It was hard work. All the day through I would be running with a drink to one or another of my three masters.

"Ye've Murdered the Boy!"

At night I slept on a blanket thrown on the deck boards of the roundhouse. But I was well fed, and I could have been drunk from morning till night, like Mr. Shuan, if I had wanted to be. I had good company in Mr. Riach, who had been to college and talked to me like a friend.

But the shadow of poor Ransome lay on all four of us, and on me and Mr. Shuan most heavily. And then I had troubles of my own. For the present, I had to serve three men I looked down upon. And as for the future, I could only see myself slaving in the tobacco fields.

David Has His Own Troubles.

Listening in the Fog

Chapter 10

The Man with the Belt of Gold

More than a week went by. The tenth afternoon there was a falling swell and a thick, wet, white fog that hid one end of the brig from the other. I felt danger in the air and was excited.

Maybe about ten at night, I was serving Mr. Riach and the captain their supper, when the ship struck something with a great sound.

"She's struck!" said Mr. Riach.

"No, sir," said the captain, "we've only run a boat down."

75

KIDNAPPED

We had run down a boat in the fog, and all her crew but one had drowned. The moment of the blow, he had leapt up and caught hold of the brig's bowsprit. That had taken luck and much strength.

The man was small, but nimble as a goat. His eyes were light and had a kind of dancing madness in them. He wore fine clothes: a feathered hat, breeches of black plush, and his coat had silver buttons. Fine clothes, but they were spoiled a bit by fog and being slept in. He laid a pair of pistols decorated with silver on the table, and I saw he wore a great sword. I thought, at first sight, that here was a man I would rather call my friend than my enemy.

They sent me for food. When I returned, the gentleman had his money belt full of gold guineas on the table, and the captain was agreeing to set him ashore at a safe place.

"Here's my hand upon it," said the captain,

The Man with the Belt of Gold

and then he left. While I served the man supper, he told me that he was a smuggler of rents and had served King Louis of France. He was a rebel against the English king, and his life would be in danger the moment he set foot on land.

When I went to get him some wine I heard Hoseason and Riach plotting against him for his money. I was filled with anger at the greedy, bloody men that I sailed with.

They called me in because they needed me to get powder and guns from the roundhouse. They knew that the stranger would not suspect me.

"I'll remember it when we come to Carolina," said Hoseason. "And David, that man has a beltful of gold, and I give you my word you shall have some of it."

What was I to do? They were dogs and thieves. They had stolen me from my country; they had killed poor Ransome. Was I to

David Overhears the Plot.

help in another murder? But what could a boy and a man do against a whole ship's company?

I returned to the roundhouse and put my hand on the man's shoulder.

"Do ye want to be killed?" said I.

He sprang to his feet.

"They're all murderers here."

"Will ye stand with me?" said he.

"That I will!" said I.

"Why, then," said he, "what's your name?"

"David Balfour," said I, "of Shaws."

"My name is Stewart," he said. "Alan Breck, they call me."

We set to securing the roundhouse. When I moved to slide shut the stout oak door, Alan stopped me.

"It would be better shut," said I.

"Not so, David," said he. "I have but one face. So long as that door is open and my face to it, my enemies will be in front of me,

80

David Warns Alan of the Plot.

where I would wish to find them. How many are against us?"

"Fifteen," said I.

Alan whistled. "Well," said he, "as soon as the pistols are charged, then ye must climb into yon bed so ye're ready at the window. If they lift a hand against that door, ye're to shout. It is my part to keep this door. And don't fire over here unless they get me down. I'd rather have ten foes in front of me than one friend cracking pistols at my back!"

Charging the Pistols

The Captain Appears at the Door.

Chapter 11

The Siege of the Roundhouse

The captain appeared in the open door.

"Stand!" cried Alan and pointed his sword at him.

Hoseason said nothing to Alan, but looked over at me with an ugly look. "David," said he, "I'll remember this," and the sound of his voice went through me. Next moment he was gone.

A little while after, there came a clash of steel upon the deck. I knew they were dealing out cutlasses and one had fallen. After that, silence again.

KIDNAPPED

It came all of a sudden when it did, with a rush of feet and a roar, then a shout from Alan, and a sound of blows and someone crying out as if hurt. I looked back over my shoulder and saw Mr. Shuan in the doorway, crossing blades with Alan.

"That's him that killed the boy!" I cried.

"Look to your window!" said Alan.

Five men took places to drive the door in. I had never fired with a pistol in my life, never against a fellow creature. But it was now or never. I cried out, "Take that!" and shot.

The whole place was full of smoke. My ears seemed to be burst with the noise of the shots. There was Alan, standing as before, only now his sword was bloody to the hilt. Right before him on the floor was Mr. Shuan. Those behind him dragged him out of the roundhouse. He was dead.

I told Alan I had winged one and thought it was the captain. Keeping watch with eye and

"Look to Your Window!"

ear, I recharged the three pistols I had fired. The thought of sharp swords and cold steel was strong in me. When I began to hear stealthy steps and knew they were taking their places in the dark, I almost cried out.

I heard seamen drop softly on the roof above me. A knot of them, cutlasses in hand, made one rush against the door. At the same moment, the glass of the skylight was dashed, and a man leapt through and landed on the floor. He grabbed me. I gave a shriek and shot him in the middle of the body. A second fellow I shot in the thigh.

The door was crowded with faces. I was thinking we were lost, when lo! Alan was driving them along the deck as a sheepdog chases sheep.

The roundhouse was a shambles. Three were dead inside, another lay dying across the doorway. Alan and I were victorious and unhurt. He came up to me with open arms.

A Seaman Grabs David.

"Come to my arms!" he cried, and embraced and kissed me hard upon both cheeks. "David," said he, "I love you like a brother. And O man, am I not a bonny fighter?"

The thought of the two men I had shot was like a nightmare, and before I had a guess of what was coming, I began to sob and cry like any child. Alan clapped my shoulder and said I was a brave lad and only needed a sleep.

He took the first watch, pistol in hand and sword on knee. Then he roused me up and I took my turn of three hours. It was then broad day and a very quiet morning. There was a smooth rolling sea that tossed the ship and made the blood run to and fro on the roundhouse floor, and a heavy rain that drummed upon the roof. I learned later that so many of the men were hurt or dead, and the rest of them in so ill a temper, that Mr. Riach and the captain had to take turns at

Alan Takes the First Watch.

the watch like Alan and me. Otherwise the brig might have drifted ashore. No one would have known because there was no one at the tiller.

No One at the Tiller

A Silver Button

Chapter 12

The Captain Knuckles Under

Alan and I sat down to breakfast at about six o'clock. We had all the drink in the ship and all the dainty food, but the broken glass and horrid mess of blood on the floor took away my hunger.

Alan, taking a knife from the table, cut off one of the silver buttons from his coat.

"I got them," said he, "from my father, Duncan Stewart, and now give ye one of them to be a keepsake for last night's work. Wherever ye go and show that button, the friends of Alan Breck will come around you."

We were hailed by Mr. Riach, asking for a parley. I climbed through the skylight and sat on the edge of it, pistol in hand. He looked out of heart and weary.

"This is a bad job," said he at last, shaking his head.

"We didn't choose it," said I.

"The captain," said he, "would like to speak with your friend."

The captain came to one of the windows and stood there in the rain, with his arm in a sling. He looked stern and pale and so old that I was sorry I had fired at him.

"Ye've made sore hash of my brig. I haven't men enough to sail her. There is nothing left me but to put back into the port of Glasgow."

"Ay?" said Alan. "Unless there's nobody who speaks English in that town, I'll have a bonny tale for them. Fifteen sailors upon one side, and a man and a halfling boy upon the other. O man, it's pitiful!"

The Captain Comes to the Window.

Hoseason flushed red. "But my first officer is dead. There's none of us who knows this coast. It's one very dangerous to ships."

It was finally decided that the captain would risk the brig to set Alan safely along the coast. The last part of the treaty was a trade: a bottle of brandy for two buckets of water. Alan and I could at last wash out the roundhouse, and the captain and Mr. Riach could be happy again in their way, with a drink.

Trading Brandy for Water

Listening to Alan's Tales

Chapter 13

I Hear of the "Red Fox"

A breeze sprang up and blew off the rain and brought out the sun. Alan and I sat in the roundhouse with the doors open and smoked a pipe or two of the captain's tobacco. We heard each other's stories, and I learned of that wild Highland country where we were soon to land. So soon after the great rebellion, a man needed to know what he was doing when he went upon the heather.

Alan told me he had been in the English army.

"What!" cried I.

"That was I," said Alan. "But I deserted."

"The punishment is death," said I.

"Ay," said he, "if they get their hands on me."

"Good heaven, man," cried I, "you are a condemned rebel, and a deserter, and a man of the French kings—what tempts ye back into this country?"

"Well, ye see, I weary for my friends and country," said he. "And then I have some things that I must attend to. Ye see, David, the English rogues tried to break the clans. They stripped the chiefs of power, land, even clothes—they say it's a sin to wear a tartan plaid. One thing they could not kill. That was the love the clansmen bore their chief. Ardshiel is the captain. The poor folk have to pay rent to King George. They scrape up a second rent for Ardshiel. David, I'm the hand that carries it to him.

"Colin Roy, of black Campbell blood," he

"I'm the Hand that Carries the Rent."

continued fiercely, "makes these poor folk pay triple for their own land. Rent to King George, then rent he knows they save for their chief, then more to him! Ah, Red Fox, if ever I hold you at a gun's end, the Lord have pity on ye!"

And with this, Alan fell into a muse and for a long time sat very sad and silent.

Very Sad and Silent

Close to the Reefs

Chapter 14

The Loss of the Brig

It was late at night.

"Here," said Hoseason at the door, "come out and see if ye can pilot."

"Is this one of your tricks?" asked Alan.

"Do I look like tricks?" cried the captain. "I have other things to think of—my brig's in danger."

The *Covenant* tore through the seas at a great rate, pitching and straining. We were close to the reefs. The captain stood by the steersman, listening and looking steady as steel. Alan was very white.

"Oh, David," said he, "this is no kind of death I like."

"What, Alan!" I cried. "You're not afraid?"

"No," said he, wetting his lips, "but you'll agree, it's a cold ending."

The tide caught the brig and threw the wind out of her sails. She came round into the wind like a top. The next moment she struck the reef and threw us all flat upon the deck. We could hear her beat herself to pieces on the rocks. The captain seemed to suffer along with her. His brig was like wife and child to him.

The wounded who could move began to help. The rest that lay helpless in their bunks screamed and begged to be saved.

All the time of our working the lifeboat, I remember only one other thing. I asked Alan what part of the shore it was, and he answered it was the worst possible for him. It was land of the Campbells.

Readying the Lifeboat

KIDNAPPED

A man sang out pretty shrill, "For God's sake, hold on!" There followed a sea so huge it lifted the brig right up and tilted her over on her beam. I was thrown clean over the bulwarks into the sea.

I was being hurled along and beaten upon and choked. Presently, I found I was holding to a mast which helped me float. I had traveled far from the brig. I hailed her, but it was plain she was already too far away. I began to feel a man could die of cold as well as drowning.

The shore was close. In about an hour of hard work, kicking and splashing, I could wade ashore by foot.

There was no sound of surf. The sea was quite quiet. The moon shone clear, and I thought in my heart I had never seen a place so alone and desolate.

Holding to a Mast to Stay Afloat

Alone in the Rain

Chapter 15

The Islet

Stepping ashore, I began the most unhappy part of my adventures. It was hours till dawn and it was cold.

At dawn, there was no sign of the brig, which must have lifted from the reef and sunk. The lifeboat was gone too. There was no sail upon the ocean and no sign of man on the land. I was afraid to think of what had happened to my shipmates, and I worried for Alan.

I was wet, tired and hungry. Instead of the sun rising to dry me, it began to rain, with a thick mist. I had nothing in my pockets but money and Alan's silver button. I found shellfish among the rocks and ate them cold and raw. At first they seemed delicious, but as long as I was on the island I never knew what to expect when I had eaten. Sometimes I got deathly sick; sometimes all was well.

The second day I walked the island. There was a creek that cut off the isle from the mainland, but it was too wide and deep to cross. I was quite alone with dead rocks, and fowls, and the rain, and the cold sea. My clothes were beginning to rot and my throat was very sore.

That day I saw a boat with a brown sail and two fishers. I shouted out and then fell to my knees and reached up my hands to them. The boat never turned aside. I could not believe such wickedness. I wished I could kill them.

The next day I saw the same boat returning.

Finding Shellfish Among the Rocks

It came within shouting range, but no closer. I was frightened because the men in it were laughing.

One spoke fast with many wavings of his hand. I told him I knew no Gaelic, and I only picked out one word he said—"tide."

"Yes, yes," he repeated. "Tide."

They laughed. I ran to the creek. The tide was out, and I crossed over easily to the mainland. The island was what they call a tidal islet and could be entered or left twice every twenty-four hours as the tide fell. I had stupidly starved with cold and hunger for almost one hundred hours. If the fishers had not returned, I might have left my bones there, like a fool.

"Tide!"

Asking the Old Gentleman

Chapter 16

The Lad with the Silver Button: Through the Isle of Mull

On the land, rugged and trackless, I had no better guide than my own nose. I came upon a house and an old gentleman who sat smoking his pipe in the sun. In broken English, he told me my shipmates had gotten safely ashore and had eaten in this same house the day before.

"Was there one," I asked, "dressed like a gentleman?"

He said the first of them, the one that came alone, wore breeches and stockings instead of sailor's clothes like the rest.

I smiled, partly because my friend was safe, partly remembering his vanity in dress. Then the old gentleman clapped his hand to his brow and cried out that I must be the lad with the silver button.

"Why, yes!" said I, in some wonder.

"Well, then," said the old gentleman, "I have a word for you. You are to follow your friend to his country, by Torosay." Then he gave me food and a place to sleep before I was on my way.

Along the road I met many grubbing in miserable fields that would not give enough food to support a cat. I could see that the English law was harshly applied. Soon after the rebellion, kilts were outlawed in hopes of breaking the clan spirit, and the men here wore strange get-ups in place of trousers.

I fought a man who tried to cheat me and took his shoes and knife when I left him. A blind man armed with a gun tried to take my

Miserable Fields

money, but I walked around him in circles, keeping myself some steps away. He cursed me and went his own way. The last man I met was a fine landlord. We talked and drank long into the night.

I had come almost one hundred miles in four days. I went to bed in far better heart and health of body at the end of that long tramp than I had been at the beginning.

Walking Circles Around the Blind Man

"I Am Seeking Somebody."

Chapter 17

The Lad with the Silver Button: Across Morven

There is a regular ferry from the mainland to Torosay. The skipper of the boat was called Neil Roy Macrob. Macrob was one of the names of Alan's clansmen, and Alan himself had sent me to the ferry, so I was eager to talk to Neil Roy.

At Kinlochaline I got Neil Roy aside and asked if he was one of Ardshiel's men.

"And what for?" said he.

"I am seeking somebody," said I. "Alan Breck Stewart is his name." I showed him the button lying in the hollow of my palm.

KIDNAPPED

"Ye are the lad with the silver button," said Neil, "and I have word to see that ye come safe. But if ye will pardon me to speak plainly," said he, "there is a name you should never speak, and that is the name of Alan Breck."

He gave me my directions quickly.

Early in the next day's journey, I overtook a stout little man walking very slowly with his toes turned out. He read from a book and was dressed as a clergyman. His name was Henderland, and he knew my old friend, Mr. Campbell, from Essendean. I told him of my adventures, but said nothing of Alan. He seemed to have heard of Alan already.

"Alan Breck is a bold, desperate customer and well-known to be James' right hand. James is half-brother to the chief, Ardshiel. Breck's here and away; here today and gone tomorrow, a regular heather cat. He might be watching the two of us out of yon bush, I

"Breck's a Regular Heather Cat."

wouldn't wonder! There's money on his head, but I hear he's a man to be respected." I thought Alan would be pleased to hear this story of himself.

Mr. Henderland also told me he feared for Colin Roy Campbell, the Red Fox. He thought the Highlands would see fighting soon.

Walking and Talking

Rough and Barren Country

Chapter 18

The Death of the Red Fox

The next day Mr. Henderland found for me a man who had a boat of his own and was going to cross the Linnhe Loch to fish. It saved me a long day's travel and the price of two public ferries.

It was near noon before we set out on a dark day with clouds. The mountains were high, rough and barren, very black and gloomy. It seemed a hard country to care as much about as Alan did.

At last we came so near the point of land that I begged to be set on shore. I sat down in a wood of birches to eat some of Mr. Henderland's oat-bread and think. I wondered why I was going to join an outlaw and a would-be murderer like Alan.

I saw four travelers come into view. The first was a great red-headed gentleman, him they call Red Fox. He asked me where I was going and why. As he turned, there came the shot of a firelock from higher up the hill. Colin Roy Campbell fell upon the road.

"Oh, I am dead!" he cried.

One of his companions caught him and held him in his arms. "I am dead," said Campbell.

The murderer was still moving away at no great distance. He was a big man in a black coat.

"Here!" I cried. "I see him."

I began running after him.

"Ten pounds if you take the lad!" cried one. "He helped the murderer. He made us stop to

The Red Fox Comes First.

talk."

My heart came to my mouth with quite a new kind of terror. I was all amazed and helpless.

"Duck in here among the trees," said a voice close by. Just inside the shelter of the trees I found Alan Breck. "Come!" said he and set off running.

We ran among birches; we crawled among the heather. The pace was deadly. My heart seemed to be bursting against my ribs.

"Now," said he, "it's earnest. Do as I do, for your life."

We traced back across the mountainside till at last Alan threw himself down in the upper wood and, lay with his face in the ferns, panting like a dog.

My own sides ached, my head swam. My tongue hung out of my mouth with heat and dryness. I lay beside him like one dead.

Finally Able to Rest

David Suspects Alan.

Chapter 19

I Talk with Alan

"Well," said he, "that was a hot chase, David."

I said nothing. I had seen murder done and a great, ruddy, jovial gentleman struck out of life in a moment. Here the man that Alan hated was murdered. Here was Alan skulking in the trees and running from the troops. The way I saw it, the only friend I had in that wild country was blood-guilty. I could not look at him.

"Are ye still wearied?" he asked again.

"No," said I, with my face still to the

ground. "You and I must part," I said. "I like ye very well, Alan, but your ways are not mine."

"I will hardly part from ye, David, without some kind of reason," said Alan very gravely.

"Alan," said I, "ye know very well yon Campbell lies in his blood, murdered."

"I will tell you, Mr. Balfour of Shaws, that if I were going to kill a gentleman, it would not be in my own country, to bring trouble on my clan." He took out his dirk and laid it on his hand in a certain manner. "I swear upon the Holy Iron I had no part nor art, act nor thought in it."

I offered him my hand. At first he would not take it. He looked at me awhile, then gave me both of his hands, saying surely I had cast a spell upon him, for he could forgive me anything. Then he grew very grave and said we both must flee that country. He, because he was a deserter, and I, because the

Alan Swears Upon the Holy Iron.

troops involved me in the murder.

"Ay, man, ye shall walk many a weary mile before we get safe. But if ye ask what other chance ye have, I answer: none. Either take to the heather with me, or else hang."

"I'll go with you, Alan," said I.

Looking out between the trees, away at the far end of the mountain, little red soldiers were dipping up and down over hill and hollow.

Alan watched them, smiling to himself. "Ay," said he, "they'll be weary before they've got to the end of that search. And so you and I, David, can sit down and eat a bite and breathe a bit longer."

Partly as we sat, and partly on the way, each of us told his adventures.

Alan had run to the bulwarks as soon as the wave was passed, and he saw me and lost me and saw me again clinging to the mast. This put some hope in him that maybe I

Little Red Soldiers in the Distance

would get to land after all. It made him leave those clues and messages which had brought me to that unlucky country of Appin.

Those still on the brig had gotten the lifeboat launched, and one or two were on board already. A second wave heaved the brig out of her place. She struck on some edge of the reef, and the water began to pour into the ship like the pouring of a dam.

Once ashore, Hoseason was after Alan for his money belt because he had lost his ship, but Riach had stood by Alan and he made a run for it.

"Ye see, there's a strip of Campbells in that end of Mull, which is no good company for a gentleman like me," said he. "If it had not been for that I would have waited and looked for ye myself and stayed to help that little man, Mr. Riach."

Riach Stood by Alan.

David and Alan See the Lights.

Chapter 20

The House of Fear

Night fell as we were walking. Alan pushed on. I could not see how he knew where he was. We came to a hilltop and saw lights below us. A house door stood open and let out a beam of fire and candlelight. Five or six persons hurried about.

"James has lost his wits," said Alan. "If we were soldiers, he would be in a bonny mess."

He whistled three times in a particular manner, and we came down the hill. We were met by a man who cried out to Alan in Gaelic.

"James Stewart," said Alan, "I will ask ye to speak in Scotch, for here is a young gentleman with me who knows no other. I am thinking it will be better for his health if we don't mention his name."

James of the Glens greeted me, then turned to Alan.

"This has been a dreadful accident," he cried. "It will bring trouble to the country."

"Hoots!" said Alan. "Colin Roy is dead, and be thankful for that!"

"Ay," said James. "It was all very fine to boast before. But now it's done, who's to bear the blame? O man, man, man, Alan! You and I have spoken like two fools!" he cried. "For with all that I have said and that you have said, it will look very black against us. Do ye mark that?"

"Ay," said Alan, "I see that."

"Alan, I have a family. And Alan, it'll be a jury of Campbells. They'll hang both of us."

146

James Speaks of the Trouble.

Each clan protected its own. James and Alan would not think of betraying the real murderer, whoever he was. Since Alan and I were suspected and on the run, it seemed we were to take the blame. There soon would be posters up for our arrest. The only hope we had was that James and his family would be safe while the law and those little red soldiers were after Alan and me.

The family gave us each a sword and pistols, some ammunition, a bag of oatmeal, an iron pan and a bottle of French brandy. We had little money; Alan's belt had been taken for other uses.

Alan turned to me and said, "Tomorrow there'll be a fine riding of soldiers and running of redcoats in Appin. You and I should be gone."

"You and I Should Be Gone."

Sometimes Walking, Sometimes Running

Chapter 21

The Flight in the Heather: The Rocks

Sometimes we walked, sometimes ran. As it became morning, we walked less and ran more. Alan stopped at houses along the way to pass the news. In that country, this was so much of a duty that Alan took the time to do it even while fleeing for his life.

We were far from shelter at the first peep of morning.

"This is no fit place for you and me," Alan said. "This is a place they're bound to watch."

With that we ran harder than ever. We came to the waterside in a part where the

151

river was split by three rocks. Alan looked neither right nor left, but jumped clean to the middle rock and fell there on his hands and knees. I followed him, and he caught and stopped me.

When I saw where I was, there came on me a deadly sickness of fear, and I put my hand over my eyes. Alan took me and shook me. Then, putting his hands to his mouth, and his mouth to my ear, he shouted, "Hang or drown!" He then leapt over the rest of the stream and landed safe. I bent low on my knees and flung myself forward, but my hands slipped. Alan seized me, first by the hair, then by the collar, and dragged me to safety.

He said nothing, but set off running again for his life. I stumbled after him. He led the way to a large rock. Alan stood on my shoulders so he could reach the top. Then he pulled me up. There was a hollow in its

Being Dragged to Safety

center where we could lie and not be seen. It was daylight now.

"Ye're not very good at the jumping," he said.

I blushed.

"Hoots! Small blame to ye! To be afraid of a thing and yet to do it is what makes the prettiest kind of a man. Go to your sleep, lad, and I'll watch."

Alan woke me roughly, pressing a hand over my mouth. I looked around. About a half a mile up the river there was a camp of redcoats. Nearby, on the top of a rock, there stood a sentry, with the sun sparkling on his gun.

I took one look and ducked down again into my place.

"Ye see," said Alan, "this was what I was afraid of, Davie."

We had to lie on the rock and hide till night. The sun beat down and the rock

A Camp of Redcoats Nearby

burned us. All the while, we had no water, only raw brandy for a drink, which was worse than nothing.

The soldiers kept moving all day in the bottom of the valley. They changed guard and formed patrolling parties that hunted among the rocks.

At about two, the sun was too hot to bear.

"As well one death as another," said Alan and slipped over the edge, dropping to the ground on the shadowy side of the rock. I followed him at once. I was weak and dizzy. We lay there for an hour or two, then began to slip from rock to rock, crawling flat on our bellies or making a run for it. A man needed a hundred eyes in every part of him to keep hidden in that country.

The moon rose at last. We were still on the road. We came to a string of mountains, and Alan seemed pleased we were safe for a bit. He must have judged that we were out of

Alan Slips over the Edge.

earshot of all our enemies. For he began whistling many tunes, warlike, merry, sad; tunes that made the feet go faster, and tunes of my own south country that made me wish to be home.

Whistling Tunes

In Front of the Cave

Chapter 22

The Flight in the Heather: A Message

We came to a valley in a great mountain, with water running down the middle and a shallow cave in the rock on one side. It was here Alan had been headed.

We slept in the cave, making our bed of heather bushes and covering ourselves with Alan's greatcoat. There was a place we could build a small fire and grill the little trouts we caught in the stream. Alan also taught me to use a sword.

On our first morning, Alan said to me, "We must get word sent to James."

"And how?" said I. "We cannot leave here. Can you get the birds to talk for you?"

He got two sticks of wood, made them into a cross, and burnt the four ends of it in the coals. Then he turned and looked at me a little shyly.

"Could ye lend me my button?" said he. "It seems strange to ask for a gift back, but I don't want to cut another." I gave him the button. He tied it to the cross and added a sprig of birch and another of fir.

"Ye see, David," said he, "I will steal down into the little village near here and set this in the window of a good friend of mine, John Breck Maccoll. He will know something is up by the cross. Then he will see my button, which was Duncan Stewart's, and know that the son of Duncan is in need of him. He will know to come to the wood of birch and pine by the sprigs I have tied to the cross."

"Eh, man," said I, teasing him, "you're very

The Cross with the Button

KIDNAPPED

smart. But wouldn't it be simpler to write a note?"

"Yes, Mr. Balfour of Shaws, but it would be a job for John Breck to read it. He would have to go to school for two or three years, and we might get tired waiting for him."

John Breck understood Alan's sign and found us. He went to James Stewart with a note, but returned with an answer from Mrs. Stewart. James was in prison. She begged Alan not to let himself be captured. The money she sent was all that she could beg or borrow. Lastly, she sent one of the notices for our arrest that described our faces and our clothes. It seemed that Alan's company was not only dangerous to my life, but would be unhealthy for my pocketbook as well.

After looking at the notices for our arrest and seeing the amount of money that was on our heads, neither of us felt very safe. Alan and I left the cave that day.

164

A Notice for Our Arrest

Crossing the Desert Land

Chapter 23

The Flight in the Heather:
The Ambush

After seven hours of hard traveling, we came to the end of a range of mountains. In front of us there lay a piece of low, broken desert land which we had to cross. Much of it was red with heather; some had been burnt black in a fire. In another place there was a forest of dead firs, standing like skeletons. Much of the rest of it was broken by bogs and swamps.

Sometimes we crawled from heather bush to heather bush for a full hour. We wore away the morning and about noon lay down in a thick bush of heather to sleep. Alan took the first watch, and it seemed to me I had only time to close my eyes before I was shaken up to take the second watch. But by this time I was so weary that I could have slept twelve hours at a stretch. I had the taste of sleep in my throat, and the humming of the wild bees was like a sleeping potion. Every now and then I would jump and find that I had been dozing.

The last time I woke I seemed to come back from farther away and thought the sun had moved far in the sky. When I looked around me on the moor, my heart sank. Soldiers were spread out in the shape of a fan, riding their horses and searching the heather.

I woke Alan. He glanced at the soldiers, then at the position of the sun, and gave me a quick look. "We'll have to play at being rabbits," said he. "Do ye see yon mountain?"

Only Time to Close My Eyes

"Ay," said I.

"Well, then," said he, "let's head for that."

"But, Alan," cried I, "that will take us across the path of the soldiers!"

"I know," said he, "but if we are taken back to Appin, we are two dead men. So now, David man, be brisk!"

Nothing but the fear of Alan gave me enough of a false kind of courage to go on. We ran and crawled, crawled and stumbled, until the sun fell. Never a word passed between us. Neither of us really looked where we were running to. It was plain that Alan must have been as stupid with weariness as I was, or we would not have walked into an ambush like blind men. The heather gave a sudden rustle, three or four ragged men leapt out, and the next moment we were lying on our backs with knives at our throats.

I heard Alan and another whispering in Gaelic. The knives were removed, our

Knives at Our Throats

weapons were taken away, and we were left sitting in the heather under guard.

"They are Cluny's men," said Alan.

Cluny Macpherson was chief of a Highland clan and had been one of the leaders in the great rebellion six years before. There was a price on his head, as there was on ours. We had been caught in his territory, but he had heard of Alan Breck, and we weren't likely to be harmed. Alan was clearly at ease. As soon as the men had set us down, he had fallen fast asleep. There was no such thing possible for me. I lay awake.

Cluny sent word that we should come to him. I was feverish, tired and hungry, and my head felt silly and light. I could not walk alone. Alan had the men half-carry me along, and I felt I was in a dream.

Under the Guard of Cluny's Men

Cluny's Cage

Chapter 24

Cluny's Cage

Just before the rocky face of the cliff could be seen above the foliage, we found that strange house which was known as "Cluny's Cage." A tree which grew out from the hillside was the living beam of the roof. Earth had been filled in along the slope to make a level floor. The walls were made of woven branches covered with moss. The whole house was shaped like an egg and was large enough to shelter five or six persons comfortably.

This was only one of Cluny's hiding places; he had caves and underground chambers in different parts of his country. He moved from one to the other as soldiers came near or moved away.

It was certainly a strange place, and we had a strange host. In his long hiding, Cluny had taken on the habits of an old maid. He had a certain place where no one else could sit, and the cage was arranged a certain way which no one could disturb.

He sometimes visited or received visits from his wife and one or two of his nearest friends at night, but for the most part he lived alone and only talked to the sentinels and the men who waited on him in the cage. Although he kept himself so alone, he still knew all the business of the clan and made the final decision on clan matters and disputes.

I remember little of the few days Alan and I spent there. I was feverish and was in bed and asleep most of the time. I do know that Cluny was suspicious of me because I would

A Strange Host

not play cards with them. My father had been very against card playing and gambling, and I shared his dislike for the game.

And I know that Alan lost all our money to Cluny in their card game. He came to me while I was half-asleep and asked for a loan. I gave it to him without thinking, and he lost it.

We were none of us talking to each other when Alan and I set out. I had told Cluny that I wouldn't take back as a gift the money he had won fairly from Alan. He returned the money because he knew he could not let two friends go out with no money when they were wanted by the law, but he was not happy to do it. Alan was quiet and feeling guilty for losing the money. I had nothing to say to either of them. I was still tired and a bit sick and wished I was alone.

Alan Loses Money at Cards.

Marching Along Saying Nothing

Chapter 25

The Flight in the Heather:
The Quarrel

For long, we said nothing. We marched along. I was angry and proud; Alan was angry and ashamed. He was ashamed that he had lost my money and angry that I should be so upset about it. I thought of leaving him, but I could not turn to a friend who certainly loved me and say, "You are in great danger, I am in little danger. Your friendship puts me in danger, so go on alone." No, that was impossible.

And yet Alan had taken my money when I was half-conscious and lost it. I was ready to share it with him, but not ready for him to lose it at cards.

For most of three nights we traveled on eerie mountains and among wild rivers. We were often buried in mist, almost continually blown and rained upon, and not once cheered by any glimpse of sunshine. It was never warm; my teeth chattered in my head. I also had a very sore throat.

During these horrid wanderings we hardly spoke. I was almost wishing I was dead. I was unforgiving by nature, slow to get angry, slower to forget it, and now furious with Alan and with myself. Sometimes he would tease me to try to make me talk. I was silent.

"David," said he, "this is no way for two friends to take a small accident. I have to say that I'm sorry, and so that's said. I have long owed ye my life, and now I owe ye money. Ye should try to make that burden light for me."

This made me feel worse. I knew I was

Alan is Sorry.

behaving badly, and now I was cruel.

Alan had stopped opposite to me, his hat cocked, his hands in his breeches pockets, his head a little to one side. He began to whistle a tune of the King's army.

"Why do ye whistle that tune, Mr. Stewart?" said I. "Is that to remind me that ye have been beaten by both sides?"

The air stopped on Alan's lips

"Do ye know that ye insult me?" said Alan, very low.

"Both the Campbells and the King's men have beaten you," said I. "You have run before them like a hare."

Alan stood quite still. "This is a pity," he said at last. "There are things said that cannot be forgotten."

"I'm not asking you to," said I. "Come on!" And drawing my sword, I fell on guard as Alan had taught me.

"David!" he cried. "I cannot draw on ye. It's

"I Cannot Draw on Ye."

murder. No, no," he kept saying, "I cannot."

At this, the last of my anger oozed all out of me, and I found myself only sick, and sorry, and blank, and wondering at myself. I remembered all of Alan's kindness and courage in the past, how he had helped and cheered me in our evil days. I thought that I had lost that good friend forever. I couldn't even tell him I was sorry for the things I had said.

The pain in my side was like a sword it was so sharp. No apology could blot out what I had said, but a cry for help might make him stay with me.

"Alan!" said I, "if ye cannot help me, I must just die here."

He started up and looked at me.

"It's true," I said.

"Can ye walk?" asked Alan.

"No," said I, "not without help. I cannot breathe right. If I die, will ye forgive me,

David Asks to Be Forgiven.

Alan? In my heart, I liked ye fine, even when I was angry."

"Don't say that!" He shut his mouth with a sob. "Let me get my arm about ye. Now lean on me hard. I'll find a house for ye, David. There should be a house that's safe nearby."

"Alan," cried I, "what makes ye so good to me? What makes ye care for such a thankless fellow?"

"I don't know," said Alan. "I thought that I liked ye because ye never argued. But now that we've yelled I like ye better!"

"Now I Like Ye Better!"

A House of Maclarens

Chapter 26

The House in Balquhidder

At the door of the first house we came to, Alan knocked, which was no very safe thing to do in this part of the Highlands. Luck was with us, for it was a house of Maclarens we found. Alan was welcome because he was a Stewart and because he was Alan Breck. His name was well known in those parts. Here I lay bedridden for no more than a week, and before a month I was able to go on the road again.

All this time Alan would not leave me though I often told him he was a fool to stay in the country, and the two or three friends that were let into our secret told him the same. He hid by day in a hole in the thicket and would come into the house to visit me at night when the coast was clear. I was always pleased to see him. Mrs. Maclaren thought nothing was good enough for him, and as Duncan, her husband, had a pair of bagpipes, this time of my recovery was quite a festival. We had music every night.

Before I left, all the people in Balquhidder knew I was there, and they knew I had come with Alan. It wasn't hard to guess that I was the other man who was wanted for the murder of the Red Fox. I had changed my clothes, but I couldn't change my age or my looks, and there were notices for our arrest everywhere. Someone brought me one to look at, and it was pinned near the foot of my bed.

But no one came to question me, and the soldiers left the house alone. So it was. Some

Alan Will Not Leave David.

folk try to keep a secret between two or three friends, but it leaks out. Among these clansmen, it is told to a whole countryside, and they will keep it secret for a century.

There was only one thing that happened worth telling. Alan almost got himself in a serious sword fight with Robin Oig. Robin was one of the sons of the notorious Rob Roy and also had the law after him. He was a Campbell. Robin came by the house close to the time of Alan's coming. Duncan and I were worried; the two would not be likely to agree with each other if they met.

On his way out, Robin met Alan coming in, and the two drew back and looked at each other like strange dogs. In no time, they were politely insulting each other and ready to draw swords. I was half out of bed to try to stop them when Duncan came between the two.

"Gentlemen," said he, "here are my pipes.

Robin and Alan Look at Each Other.

You both claim to be great pipers. Here's a chance to find out which one of ye's the best." The two enemies were still on the edge of a fight, but down they sat, one on each side of the fire, with a mighty show of politeness.

It wasn't long before Robin Oig had charmed us all with his blowing and warbling on the pipes. Then all night long the music was going and the pipes were changing hands. The new day had become pretty bright before Robin even thought about leaving.

Music All Night Long

All of Stirling Below

Chapter 27

End of the Flight:
We Pass the Forth

It was already far through August, and it was beautiful warm weather. We were now in a hurry. If we didn't come to Mr. Rankeillor's soon to claim my inheritance, or if when we came there he wouldn't help us, we would starve. Alan thought the hunt after us must have let off by now and that we might be able to cross the Stirling Bridge with little trouble.

It was on a warm night when we came to the edge of the hills and saw all of Stirling below, as flat as a pancake. The town and castle were on a hill in the middle of it, and the moon was shining on the Forth River.

"Now," said Alan, "I do not know if ye care, but ye're in your own land again. We passed the Highland line in the first hour. If we could but pass yon crooked water, we'd be home free."

We waited till the night grew darker and then moved to the narrow bridge. It looked like the very doors of Salvation to Alan and me. I was for going straight across, but Alan was more careful. We hid and listened as an old hobbling woman with a crutch stick crossed the bridge. And just then—"Who goes?" cried a voice, and we heard the butt of a musket rattle on the stones. There was a guard on the bridge.

"This'll never do," said Alan. "This'll never, never do for us, David."

He began to crawl away through the fields and then struck along a road that led east.

A Guard at the Bridge

Just a moment back, I had seen myself knocking at Mr. Rankeillor's door like a hero in a ballad, and here I was again, wandering, hunted, and on the wrong side of the water.

Alan was moving toward the inlet, as wide as a sea. I argued that it would be easier to cross the river.

"How," said he, "when all the bridges and fords are watched?"

"Well," said I, "a river can be swum."

"I have yet to hear that either you or me is much good at that. I swim like a stone." Then he said, "There's such a thing as a boat."

"Ay, and money to pay for one. We have no money and no boat, so forget both," said I.

"David," said he, "ye're a man of little invention and less faith. If we cannot beg, borrow, or steal a boat, I'll make one!"

"Then," said I, "we have a boat left on the wrong side of the river. Someone will guess who brought it."

Still on the Wrong Side of the Water

"Man!" cried Alan. "If I make a boat, I'll make a body to take it back again."

To be sure, Alan did both. He made me pretend I was tired and ill, and Prince Charlie himself! The young lass at the inn where we stopped believed our game and told us that she would help if she could. She would try to find a way across the inlet for us. Alan's tale had gotten us what we needed.

We hid in a nearby wood and waited for the end of day. It was past eleven at night, and we were worried that something had gone wrong. Then we heard the grinding of oars in the rowing pins. We looked out and saw the lass herself rowing to us in a boat. She had trusted no one else, but had stolen a neighbor's boat and had come alone when everyone was asleep.

After she was gone, we had nothing to say for such a kindness. Alan stood a long while upon the shore, shaking his head.

David Pretends He Is Ill.

"It is a very fine lass," he said at last. "David, it is a very fine lass." I didn't say anything. She was such a fine lass, and I feared that we had involved her in the dangers of our own situation.

A Very Fine Lass

Teaching David the Highland Tune

Chapter 28

I Come to Mr. Rankeillor

The next day it was agreed that Alan should do for himself until sunset, but as soon as it began to grow dark, he should lie in the fields by the roadside and stay there until he heard me whistling. For our signal, he taught me a little bit of a Highland tune, which has run in my head to this day and will probably run in my head when I lie dying. Every time I hear it, I remember Alan sitting, whistling and beating the measure with a finger, and the grey of dawn coming on his face.

I was on my way through Queensferry before the sun was up. I felt like a beggar in my tattered clothes, and though I saw many people, I asked no one for directions to the lawyer's house until late afternoon.

The very man I spoke to happened to be Mr. Rankeillor himself. He led me to a little, dusty room full of books and documents, and we began our long talk.

It seemed my name had been spoken often in his office while I was away. My friend Mr. Campbell had come looking for me. My uncle swore that I had taken some money from him and set off for Europe. Mr. Rankeillor added with a small smile that no one had quite believed my uncle's story. Then Captain Hoseason had shown up with the story of my drowning in the shipwreck, and the case of my disappearance was closed. They all thought I was dead.

Then it was my turn to tell tales. I told the

Arriving at the Lawyer's House

lawyer my long story. He asked me to give different names to all the Highland men I had met. Many of them were wanted by the King's men, and Mr. Rankeillor was afraid for the safety of all of us if my story became known to others. When I mentioned Alan's name he became very nervous and insisted that I call him "Mr. Thompson" instead.

When I was finished, he reviewed my adventures, and I could see that he was not only glad that I was alive and well, but also that he was proud of me as well. He said that he thought this Mr. Thompson a good companion and a gentleman, but much too ready to fight.

I had been wandering and sleeping on hills under the bare sky for so long that I thought it fine to sit once more in a clean covered house. My clothes were in tatters, but Mr. Rankeillor seemed to understand.

He rose, called to a servant to lay another

The Lawyer Listens to David's Story.

plate because Mr. Balfour was staying for dinner, and led me to a bedroom in the upper part of the house. Here he set before me water, soap and a comb, and laid out some clothes that belonged to his son. He then left me to myself, saying that we would decide our next action over dinner.

Near the End of David's Troubles

Mr. Rankeillor Begins the Story.

Chapter 29

I Go to Claim My Inheritance

"Sit ye down, Mr. David," said Rankeillor. "You will be wondering, no doubt, about your father and your uncle? Oh, it is a tale! The matter began with a love affair," he said with a real blush.

"The two lads, your father and your uncle, fell in love with the same lady. Mr. Ebenezer, who was spoiled terribly, thought he would win her because he usually got what he wanted. But the lass loved your father. Well, Mr. Ebenezer carried on for a time. In the end the two brothers made a bargain; the one man took the lady, the other the house. Your mother and father lived and died poor folk, and Mr. Ebenezer was not so well off for all his money. He was selfish when he was young, and he has only grown more selfish each year. It was him that stopped the building of the house because he thought it was a waste of money. And he's not well liked by anyone. Those who knew the story wouldn't speak to Ebenezer, and those who only knew that your father suddenly disappeared thought he'd been murdered."

"Well, sir," said I, "what is my position now?"

"The house is yours without a doubt," said the lawyer. "My advice is to make an easy bargain with your uncle. Leave him at Shaws for a time while you take a fair allowance every month."

We agreed on a plan to outwit my uncle and set off toward Shaws. I whistled the

Good News from the Lawyer

Highland tune for Alan (or Mr. Thompson, as Mr. Rankeillor insisted on naming him), and the three of us, along with the lawyer's clerk, walked on.

I told Alan of the part he was to play in fooling my uncle. It cheered him up after the long day he had spent alone hiding.

It was night when we came to the house. It seemed my uncle was already in bed. We made our last whispered plans. Then Rankeillor, the clerk and I crept quietly up and hid by the corner of the house. As soon as we were hidden, Alan stepped up to the door and began to knock.

Last Whispered Plans

Alan Beats on the Door.

Chapter 30

I Come into My Own

For a long time Alan beat on the door, and his knocking only woke echoes in the house. At last I heard a window being opened, and I knew my uncle could see Alan standing in a shadow on the steps. He could not see us in the bush.

"What's this?" said he. "What brings ye here? I have a blunderbuss."

"Is that yourself, Mr. Balfour?" returned Alan. "Be careful with that blunderbuss. They're nasty when they go off."

"What brings ye here?" said my uncle

angrily.

"What brings me here is more your affair than mine," said Alan. "If ye would like, I'll set it to a tune and sing it to you."

"And what is it?" asked my uncle.

"David," said Alan.

The moment Alan mentioned my name, my uncle's voice changed. "I'm thinking I'd better come down," said he.

It took him a long time to get downstairs and still longer to undo all the locks and bars on the door. At last, we heard the creak of hinges. My uncle slipped out and sat down on the top doorstep with the blunderbuss ready in his hands.

Alan stood back a pace or two. He pretended that friends of his held me in a castle to the north and were demanding a money ransom.

My uncle cleared his throat. "I do not care," said he. "He was not a good lad at the best

Ebenezer and the Blunderbuss

times. I take no interest in him, and I'll pay no ransom. Do whatever ye will with him," said he.

"In two words," said Alan, "do ye want the lad killed or kept?"

"Oh, sir!" cried Ebenezer. "That's no kind of language. Oh, sirs, me!"

"Killed or kept?" repeated Alan.

"O free him!" wailed my uncle.

"Well, well," said Alan, "now about the price. I would have to know what ye gave Hoseason the first time around."

"Hoseason!" cried my uncle. "What for?"

"For kidnapping David," said Alan.

"It's a lie, it's a black lie!" cried my uncle. "He was never kidnapped. He lied in his throat that told ye that."

"Why, Hoseason himself told me," cried Alan. "We're partners. What exactly did ye pay him?"

"Well," said my uncle, "I do not care what

"Killed or Kept?"

he said, he lied, and the God's truth is this, that I gave him twenty pound. He was to sell the lad in Carolina and get the money for that too."

"Thank you, Mr. Thompson, that will do," said Mr. Rankeillor, stepping up.

And, "Good evening, Uncle Ebenezer," said I.

And, "It's a fine night, Mr. Balfour," said the clerk.

My uncle said nothing, but just sat where he was and stared upon us like a man turned to stone. Alan took away the blunderbuss, and the lawyer took my uncle's arm and led him into the kitchen.

I set myself to building a better fire while the clerk began taking a good supper from the basket he had brought. A bottle of wine was brought up from the cellar, and Alan, the clerk and I sat down to eat while the lawyer and my uncle talked in the library near the

Like a Man Turned to Stone

kitchen. After an hour, they had agreed that I would receive two-thirds of the estate.

That night Alan and Rankeillor and the clerk slept and snored on their hard beds. I lay till dawn, looking at the fire and planning the future.

David Cannot Sleep.

David Makes Plans to Help Alan.

Chapter 31

Good-Bye

The next morning at about six, Rankeillor and I walked back and forth before the house of Shaws and talked. I was wondering how I could take care of Alan. I had to help him out of the country at whatever risk.

The lawyer wrote me a letter that I was to take to his bankers for the needed money. Alan and I would decide on the best way for him to go.

Then Rankeillor left for the ferry with his clerk, and Alan and I turned our faces for the city of Edinburgh. As we went by the footpath and the unfinished gate, we took a last look back at the house.

In Edinburgh, I was to find a certain lawyer who was an Appin Stewart and could be trusted. It was his job to find a ship and arrange for Alan's safe journey. Alan was to stay in the county at different places, but come once a day to a certain place where a messenger could meet him and tell him when he was to leave.

Alan and I went slowly on our way, having little heart either to walk or speak. We both thought of our parting and remembered all the days we had been together. We tried to joke with each other, but we were both nearer tears than laughter.

We came over the hill, and when we got near the place called Rest-And-Be-Thankful and looked down over the city and the castle on the hill, we stopped. We both knew without a word said that we had come to where

Little Heart to Walk or Speak

our ways parted.

"Well, good-bye," said Alan, and he held out his left hand.

"Good-bye," said I and gave the hand a little grasp and went off down the hill.

Neither of us looked the other in the face. I didn't turn around and take one look at the friend I was leaving. As I went back to the city, I felt so lost and lonesome that I could have sat down and cried like any baby.

It was coming near noon when I found the lawyer's house. We sat down and arranged for Alan's safe trip.

Good-Bye for the Last Time